JAMES

PERCY

MEET ALL THESE FRIENDS IN BUZZ BOOKS:

Thomas the Tank Engine
The Animals of Farthing Wood
Biker Mice from Mars
Winnie-the-Pooh
Fireman Sam
Rupert
Babar

First published in Great Britain 1995 by Buzz Books,
an imprint of Reed Children's Books
Michelin House, 81 Fulham Road, London SW3 6RB
and Auckland, Melbourne, Singapore and Toronto

Photographs by David Mitton and Terry Permane for Britt Allcroft's
production of Thomas the Tank Engine and Friends

ISBN 1 855 91493 X

Printed in Italy by Olivotto

JAMES AND THE BEES

buzz books

Trevor the Traction Engine was enjoying his work in the Vicarage orchard.

Birds were singing and apples were ripening on the trees. It was a lovely day.

"Hello Trevor," said James. "You look as bright and cheerful as my red paint."

"Oh I am," replied Trevor.

"What's that noise?" asked James.

"It's the bees!" laughed Trevor. "They're all in these boxy things called beehives. I'm taking them to the station. The Vicar says his bees make good honey and is giving some of them to his friends."

Just then, Boco the Diesel Engine hummed in.

"Take care you two. Don't make the bees angry—they might sting you."

James didn't like being told what to do by a diesel and he buzzed away.

"Goodbye Trevor," called Boco, and set off to see Duck at the next station.

Bill and Ben, the tank engine twins, were busy arranging trucks but they scampered off when they saw Boco.

"I remember the first time I met those two," laughed Boco. "They nearly made my eyes pop out. Edward soon put a stop to their games."

"Edward is the only one who can keep Bill and Ben in order," chuckled Duck. "I sometimes call them 'the bees'."

"A good name," replied Boco. "They're terrors when they start buzzing around."

James bustled in.

"What's that, Duck," he snorted. "Are you afraid of bees? They're only insects after all so don't let that buzz-box diesel tell you different."

"His name is Boco and he didn't. We ... "

"I wouldn't care," interrupted James, "if hundreds were swarming around. I'd just blow smoke and make them buzz off."

"Buzz, buzz, buzz," retorted Duck.

The next morning James arrived at the station to collect his coaches. The passengers were excited and keen to get on board. The platform was crowded and the porter was in a hurry.

"Mind your backs," he shouted.

Then there was trouble!

The beehive fell and broke open.

The station cleared like magic.

James heard a familiar buzzing.

The bees were too cold to be cross so they buzzed around the fireman hoping he'd mend their hive. But he didn't understand. Nor did his driver.

So the bees turned to James.
His boiler was nice and warm.
"Buzz off, buzz off," hissed James.

One bee burnt his foot. "Oooh, aah ... phew ... !" The bee thought James had burnt him on purpose.

So it stung James right back on the nose.

"Eeeeeh!" whistled James.

He had had enough. So had his fireman and driver.

They didn't notice till too late that they had left all their coaches behind.

They tried everything to get rid of the bees.

First, they spun on the turntable, but to no avail.

They tried washing them off, but the bees clung harder to James's warm boiler.

Then they tried smoking them off by going through a long tunnel...

But still the bees wouldn't go away.

"It's no good James," said his driver. "We'll just have to go back to the orchard and fetch another hive."

James's reply was drowned by the sound of buzzing.

The Vicar was waiting anxiously for James. When he arrived the bees swarmed straight into their new home.

"Come on James," said his driver. "What you need now is a good hose down."

Later that evening James was resting in the shed when the Vicar came to see him.

“Thank you for saving my bees,” he said. “It’s a pity it’s not Christmas, then we could call you James the Red Nosed Engine.”

Everyone laughed, even James.

But instead they decided to call James "The Bees-Knees", which means they thought he was more Useful than ever.

THOMAS
1

EDWARD
2

GORDON
4